Santa Claus' Helpers

and other Christmas Stories

Miles Kelly

First published in 2015 by Miles Kelly Publishing Ltd
Harding's Barn, Bardfield End Green, Thaxted, Essex, CM6 3PX, UK

This edition printed 2018

4 6 8 10 9 7 5 3

Publishing Director Belinda Gallagher
Creative Director Jo Cowan
Editorial Director Rosie Neave
Senior Editor Sarah Parkin
Design Manager Joe Jones
Production Elizabeth Collins, Jennifer Brunwin-Jones
Reprographics Stephan Davis, Jennifer Cozens, Thom Allaway
Assets Lorraine King

ISBN 978-1-78209-827-0

Printed in China

British Library Cataloguing-in-Publication Data
A catalogue record for this book is available from the British Library

ACKNOWLEDGEMENTS
The publishers would like to thank the following artists who have contributed to this book:

Front cover: Simona Sanfilippo (Plum Pudding Illustration Agency)

Inside illustrations:
Decorative frame Rachel Cloyne (Pickled Ink)
The Nutcracker and the Mouse King Simona Sanfilippo (Plum Pudding Illustration Agency)
Santa Claus' Helpers Antonia Woodward (Plum Pudding Illustration Agency)
How Johnny Cricket Saw Santa Claus Natalia Moore (Advocate Art)

Made with paper from a sustainable forest

www.mileskelly.net

Contents

The Nutcracker and the Mouse King

Adapted from a story
by Hoffmann

*Fritz and Marie have a godfather who
always brings them wonderful presents.*

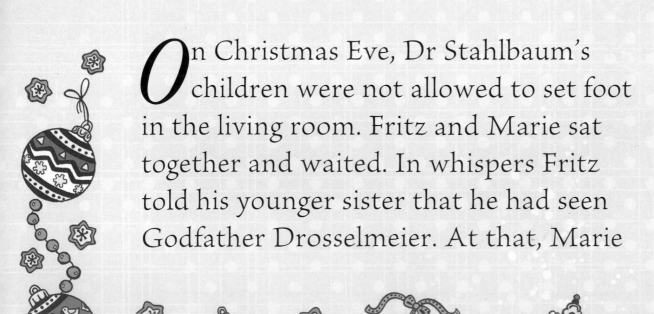

On Christmas Eve, Dr Stahlbaum's children were not allowed to set foot in the living room. Fritz and Marie sat together and waited. In whispers Fritz told his younger sister that he had seen Godfather Drosselmeier. At that, Marie clapped her hands and cried, "Oh, what do you think Godfather Drosselmeier has made for us?"

At that moment, a bell rang, the doors flew open and a flood of light streamed in.

"Come in children," said Papa and Mama.

The children stood silently with shining eyes. Then Marie found a silk dress hanging on the tree, and Fritz reviewed his new squadron of soldiers, who were fitted in red and gold uniforms.

Just then, the bell rang again. Knowing that Godfather Drosselmeier would be unveiling his present, the children ran to the table that had been set up beside the wall. The screen that had hidden it was taken away. Then the children saw a magnificent castle with dozens of sparkling windows and golden towers. Chimes played as tiny

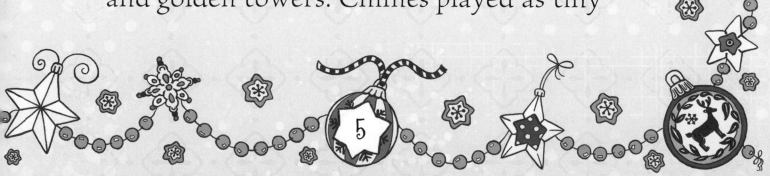

ladies and gentlemen strolled around, and children in little skirts danced.

Fritz said, "Godfather Drosselmeier, let me go inside your castle."

"Impossible," said Mr Drosselmeier.

"Then I don't really care for it," said Fritz. "My squadron of soldiers are not shut up in a castle."

Marie did not want to leave the Christmas table as she had just caught sight of something. When Fritz marched away, Marie noticed a little wooden man.

"Oh, Father dear," Marie cried out, "who does the dear little man belong to?"

"Dear child," said Dr Stahlbaum, "he belongs to us. He will crack hard nuts for you with his teeth."

Dr Stahlbaum lifted his wooden cloak, and the little man opened his mouth wide.

6

Marie put in a nut and – *crack* – the little man bit it in two, the shell fell down and Marie found the kernel in her hand.

Fritz ran over to his sister. He chose the biggest nut, and all of a sudden – *crack, crack* – three little teeth fell out of the Nutcracker's mouth.

"Oh, my poor little Nutcracker!" Marie cried.

"He's just a stupid fool," said Fritz. "He calls himself a nutcracker, but his teeth are no good."

"No, no!" Marie cried. "He's my dear Nutcracker." Sobbing, Marie wrapped the little man in her handkerchief.

Marie's mother put out all of the candles, leaving on only one lamp. "Go to bed soon," she said, "or you won't be able to get up tomorrow morning."

As soon as Marie was alone, she looked at the Nutcracker.

"Dear Nutcracker," she said softly. "I'm going to take care of you until you're well and happy again."

Marie placed him next to the other toys in a glass cabinet in the living room. She shut the door and was going to her bedroom, when she heard whispering and

8

shuffling. The clock whirred twelve times. Then she heard giggling and squeaking all around her, followed by the sound of a thousand little feet scampering behind the walls. Soon Marie saw mice all over the room, and in the end they formed ranks.

At the same time, Marie saw a strange glow inside the toy cabinet. All at once, the Nutcracker jumped from the cabinet.

"Trusty Drummer," cried the Nutcracker, "sound the advance!"

All the boxes containing Fritz's army burst open. Soldiers climbed out and jumped to the bottom shelf. Then they formed ranks on the floor.

A few moments later, guns were going *boom! boom!* The mice advanced and overran some of the artillery positions. Both sides fought with grim determination, and

for a long while victory hung in the balance.
But then the mice brought up more troops.

The Nutcracker was in dire peril. He
tried to jump over the ledge of the toy
cabinet, but his legs were too short.

At that moment, the Mouse King

charged the Nutcracker. Without quite knowing what she was doing, Marie took off her left shoe and flung it with all her might. At that moment, everything vanished from Marie's sight. She fell to the floor in a faint.

When Marie awoke from her deep sleep, she was lying in her own little bed.

"Oh, Mother dear," Marie whispered. "Have all the nasty mice gone away? Was the Nutcracker saved?"

"Don't talk such nonsense, child," said Marie's mother. "What have mice got to do with the Nutcracker?"

"Oh, Mother," Marie broke in. "There was a big battle between the dolls and the mice. The mice were going to capture the Nutcracker. So I threw my shoe at the mice, and after that I don't know what happened."

Then Godfather Drosselmeier came to

visit. "I've brought you something," he told Marie. He reached into his pocket and took out the Nutcracker, who he had fixed as good as new. Marie cried out for joy!

That night, Marie was awakened in the moonlight by a strange rumbling. Then she saw the Mouse King squeeze through the hole in the wall. He jumped onto the table beside Marie's bed.

"Give me your candy," he said, "or I'll bite your Nutcracker to pieces." Then he slipped back into the hole.

Marie was so frightened that she could hardly say a word. That night she put her whole supply of sweet things at the foot of the toy cabinet. The next morning the candy was gone.

Marie was happy because she had saved the Nutcracker, but that night the Mouse

King returned.

"Give me your beautiful dress and all your picture books," he hissed.

The next morning Marie went to the toy cabinet sobbing, and said to the Nutcracker, "Oh dear, what can I do? If I give that horrid Mouse King all my books and my dress, he'll just keep asking for more."

The Nutcracker said in a strained whisper, "Just get me a sword." At that his words ebbed away, and his eyes became fixed.

Marie asked Fritz for a sword, and Fritz slung it around the Nutcracker's waist.

The next night at the stroke of twelve, Marie heard clanging and crashing in the parlour. And then suddenly she heard a loud *squeak!*

Soon Marie heard a soft knocking at the door and a faint little voice.

"Miss Stahlbaum, open the door and have no fear. I bring good news!"

Marie very swiftly opened the door and found that the Nutcracker had turned into a prince!

The prince took Marie's hand and told her how he was really Godfather Drosselmeier's nephew, and an evil spell had turned him into a nutcracker. He said that when he defeated the Mouse King, the spell had broken and he was turned back into a prince again.

Marie fell to the floor. When she opened

her eyes, she was lying in her little bed, and her mother was standing there.

"How can anyone sleep so long!" her mother exclaimed.

One day Marie's mother came into her room and said, "Your godfather's nephew from Nuremberg is here. So be sure to be on your best behaviour."

Marie turned as red as a beetroot when she saw the young man.

He went down on one knee and said, "Miss Stahlbaum, you see at your feet the happiest of men, whose life you saved on this very spot. Please come and reign with me over Marzipan Castle."

Marie said softly, "Of course I will come with you."

Then she left in a golden carriage.

And Marie is still the queen of a country

where the most wonderful things can be seen, as long as you have the right sort of eyes to see them.

Santa Claus' Helpers

An extract from *The Life and Adventures of Santa Claus*
by L Frank Baum

*In this story about Santa Claus, he has four magical
helpers called Kilter, Peter, Nuter and Wisk.*

One Christmas Eve, when his reindeer
had leapt to the top of a new building,
Santa Claus was surprised to find that the
chimney had been built much smaller than
usual. But he had no time to think about it
just then, so he drew in his breath and made
himself as small as possible, and slid down

the chimney.

'I ought to be at the bottom by this time,' he thought, as he continued to slip downwards. But no fireplace of any sort met Santa Claus' view, and by and by he reached the very end of the chimney, which was in the cellar.

"This is odd!" he reflected, much puzzled by the experience. "If there is no fireplace, what on earth is the chimney good for?"

Then he began to climb out again and found it hard work – the space being so small. And on Santa Claus' way up he noticed a thin, round pipe sticking through the side of the chimney, but he could not guess what it was for.

Finally he reached the roof and said to the reindeer,

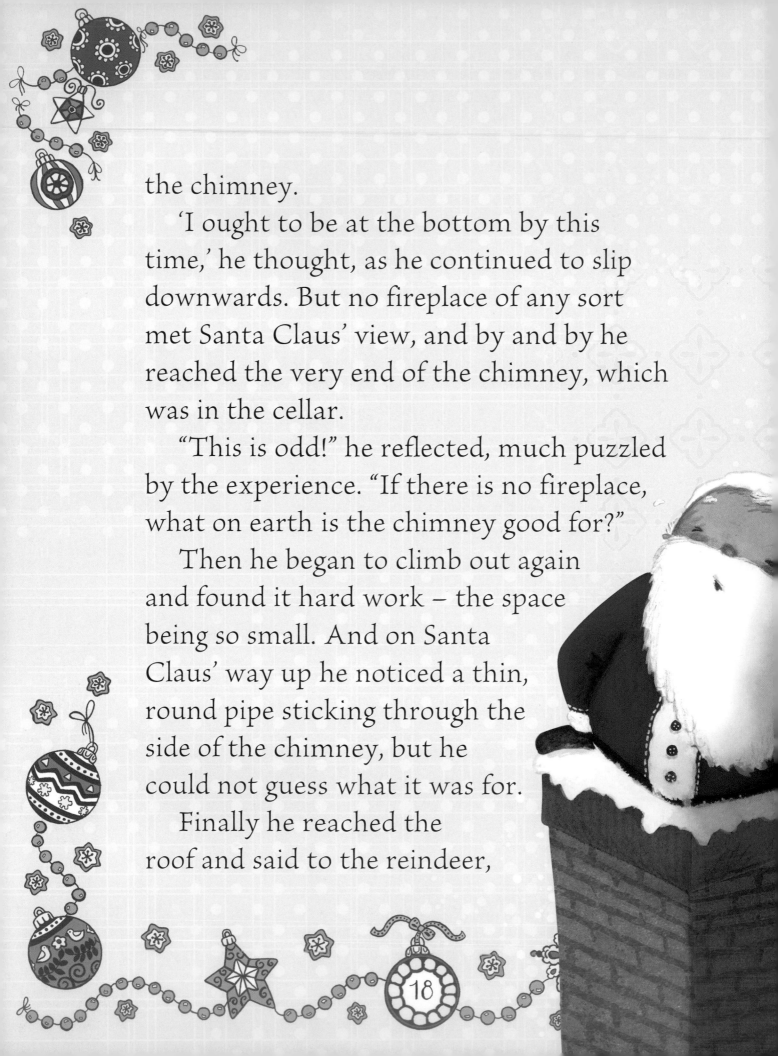

18

"There was no need of my going down that chimney, for I could find no fireplace through which to enter the house. I fear the children who live there must go without playthings this Christmas."

Santa Claus had not then discovered that stoves had been invented and were fast coming into use.

The following year Santa Claus found more and more of the new-fashioned chimneys that had no fireplaces, and the next year still more. The third year, so numerous had the narrow chimneys become, he even had a few toys left in his sledge that he was unable to give away, because he could not get to the children.

The matter had now become so serious that it worried the good man greatly, and he decided to talk it over with Kilter, Peter,

Nuter and Wisk.

Kilter already knew something about it. It had been his duty to run around to all the houses, just before Christmas, and gather up the notes and letters to Santa Claus that the children had written, telling him what they wished to be put in their stockings or hung on their Christmas trees.

"Well," declared the laughing Wisk, "we must abandon any thought of using these new-fashioned chimneys, but become burglars, and break into the houses some other way."

"What way?" asked Santa Claus.

"Why, walls of brick and wood and plaster are nothing to fairies," said Wisk. "I can easily pass through them whenever I wish, and so can Peter and Nuter and Kilter. Is it not so, comrades?"

"I often pass through the walls when I gather up the letters," said Kilter.

"Therefore," continued the fairy, "you may as well take us with you on your next journey. And when we come to one of those houses with stoves instead of fireplaces, we will distribute the toys to the children without the need of using a chimney."

"That seems to me a good plan," replied Santa Claus, well pleased at having solved the problem. "We will try it next year."

That was how the four helpers all rode in the sledge with their master the following Christmas Eve. And they had no trouble at all in entering the new-fashioned houses and leaving toys for the children that lived in them.

Taken all together, the trip was a great success, and to this day the four little

helpers always accompany Santa Claus on his yearly ride, and help him to distribute his gifts.

And Santa Claus soon found that parents were really anxious he should visit their homes on Christmas Eve and leave presents for their children. So, to lighten his task, which was fast becoming very difficult indeed,

even with his four helpers, Santa Claus
decided to ask the parents to assist him.

"Get your Christmas trees all ready for
my coming," he said to them. "And then
I shall be able to leave the presents
    without loss of time, and you can put
them on the trees when I am gone."
    And to others he said, "See that the
children's stockings are hung up in
    readiness for my coming, and then I
can fill them as quick as a wink."

And often, when parents were kind and
good-natured, Santa Claus would simply
fling down his package of gifts and leave
the fathers and mothers to fill the stockings
after he had darted away in his sledge.

"I will make all loving parents my
deputies," cried the jolly old fellow, "and
they shall help me do my work. For in this

way I shall save many precious minutes and no children need be neglected for lack of time to visit them."

Besides carrying around the big packs in his swift-flying sledge, Santa Claus began to send great heaps of toys to the toy shops, so that if parents wanted larger supplies for their children they could easily get them. And if any children were, by chance, missed by Santa Claus on his yearly rounds, they could go to the toy shops and get enough to make those children happy and contented.

Perhaps you will now understand how, in spite of the size of the world, Santa Claus is able to supply all the children with beautiful gifts. To be sure, the old gentleman is rarely seen these days. But it is not because he tries to keep out of sight, I assure you. You see, he is so busy all year making toys, and

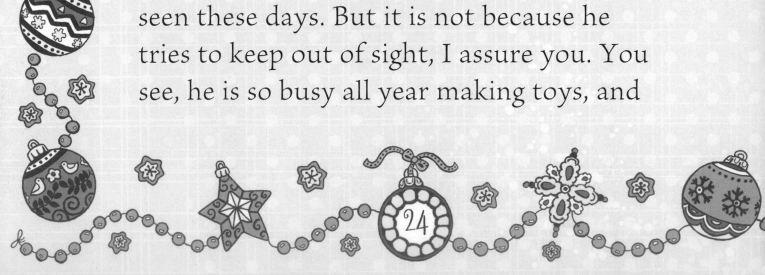

so hurried on that one night when he visits our homes with his packs, that he comes and goes among us like a flash. It is almost impossible to catch a glimpse of him.

And, although there are millions more children in the world than there used to be, Santa Claus has never been known to complain of their increasing numbers.

"The more the merrier!" he cries, with a jolly laugh. The only difference is that his little workmen have to make their busy fingers fly faster every year to satisfy.

"In all this world there is nothing so beautiful as a happy child," says Santa Claus. And if he had his way children would all be beautiful, for all would be happy.

How Johnny Cricket Saw Santa Claus

An extract from *Friendly Fairies*
by Johnny Gruelle

When the first frost came and coated the leaves with its film of sparkles, Mamma Cricket, Papa Cricket, Johnny Cricket and Grandpa Cricket decided it was time to move into their winter home.

Papa, Mamma and Grandpa Cricket carried all the heavy cricket furniture, while Johnny Cricket carried the lighter things, such as the family portraits, looking glasses,

knives and forks and spoons, and his own little violin.

Aunt Katy Didd wheeled Johnny's little sister Teeny in the baby buggy, and helped Mamma Cricket lay the rugs and wash the stonework. For the Crickets' winter home was in the chimney of a big old-fashioned house, and the walls were very dusty and everything was topsy-turvy.

But Mamma Cricket and Aunt Katy Didd soon had everything in tip-top order, and the winter home was just as clean and neat as the summer home out under the rose bush had been.

There the Cricket family lived happily, and everything was just as cosy as any little bug would care to have. On cold nights the people who owned the great big old-fashioned house always made a fire in

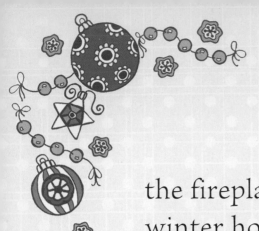

the fireplace, so the walls of the Crickets' winter home were nice and warm. Little Teeny Cricket could play on the floor in her bare feet without fear of catching cold and getting the cricket croup.

There was one crack in the walls of the Crickets' winter home that opened right into the fireplace, so the light from the fire always lit up the Crickets' living room. Papa Cricket could read the *Bugville News*, while Johnny Cricket fiddled all the latest popular bug songs, and Mamma Cricket rocked and sang to Teeny Cricket.

One night, though, the people who owned the great big old-fashioned house did not have a fire in the fireplace. Little Teeny Cricket was bundled up in warm covers and rocked to sleep, and all the Cricket family went to bed in the dark.

Johnny Cricket had just dozed into dreamland when he was awakened by something pounding ever so loudly. He slipped out of bed and into his two little red boots, and felt his way to the crack in the living room wall.

Johnny heard loud voices and merry peals of laughter, so he crawled through the crack and looked out into the fireplace.

There in front of the fireplace he saw four pink feet and two laughing faces way above, while just a couple of cricket hops from Johnny's nose was a great big man.

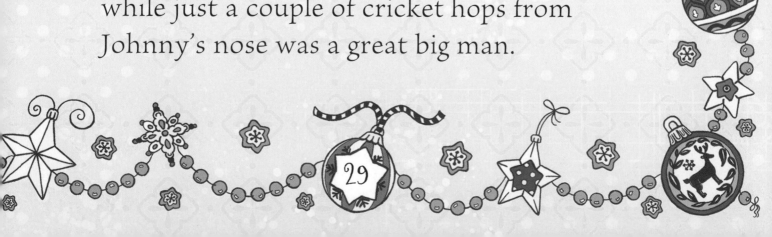

Then there were a few more squeals of laughter, and the four pink feet pitter-patted across the floor, and Johnny could see the owners hop into a snow-white bed.

Johnny saw the man walk to the lamp and turn the light down low, then leave the great big room.

Johnny Cricket jumped out of the crack into the fireplace, and ran out into the great big room. The light from the lamp was too dim for him to make out the objects that were hanging from the mantel above the fireplace. All he could see were four long black things.

So Johnny Cricket climbed up the bricks at the side of the fireplace until he came to the mantel shelf, then he ran along the shelf and looked over. He saw that the black things were stockings.

How Johnny Cricket Saw Santa Claus

Johnny began to wish that he had stopped to put on his stockings, for he had bare feet. He had removed his little red boots when he decided to climb up the side of the fireplace, and now his little feet were very cold.

So Johnny Cricket started to climb over the mantel shelf and down the side of the fireplace. And then suddenly there came a great puff of wind down the chimney that made the stockings swing away out into the room, and snowflakes fluttered clear across the room.

There was a tiny tinkle from a bell and, just as Johnny hopped behind the clock, he saw a boot stick out of the fireplace.

Then Johnny Cricket's little bug heart went *pitty-pat,* and sounded as if it would run a race with the ticking of the clock.

From his hiding place, Johnny Cricket heard one or two chuckles, and something rattle. He crept along the edge of the clock and, holding the two feelers over his back, looked from his hiding place.

At first all he could see were two hands filling the stockings with rattly things, but when the hands went down below the mantel for more rattly things, Johnny Cricket saw a big round smiling face, all fringed with snow-white whiskers.

Johnny drew back into the shadow of the clock and stayed there until all had grown quiet. Then he slipped from behind the clock and climbed down the side of the fireplace as fast as he could. Johnny Cricket was too cold to stop and put on his little red boots, but scrambled through the crack in the fireplace and hopped into bed.

In the morning, Mamma Cricket had a hard time getting Johnny out of bed. He yawned and stretched, put on one stocking, rubbed his eyes, yawned, put on another stocking and yawned again. He was still very sleepy and could hardly keep his eyes open as he reached for his little red boots.

Johnny's toe struck something hard, he yawned, rubbed his eyes and looked into the boot. Yes, there was something in Johnny Cricket's boot! He picked up the other boot. It, too, had something in it!

It was candy!

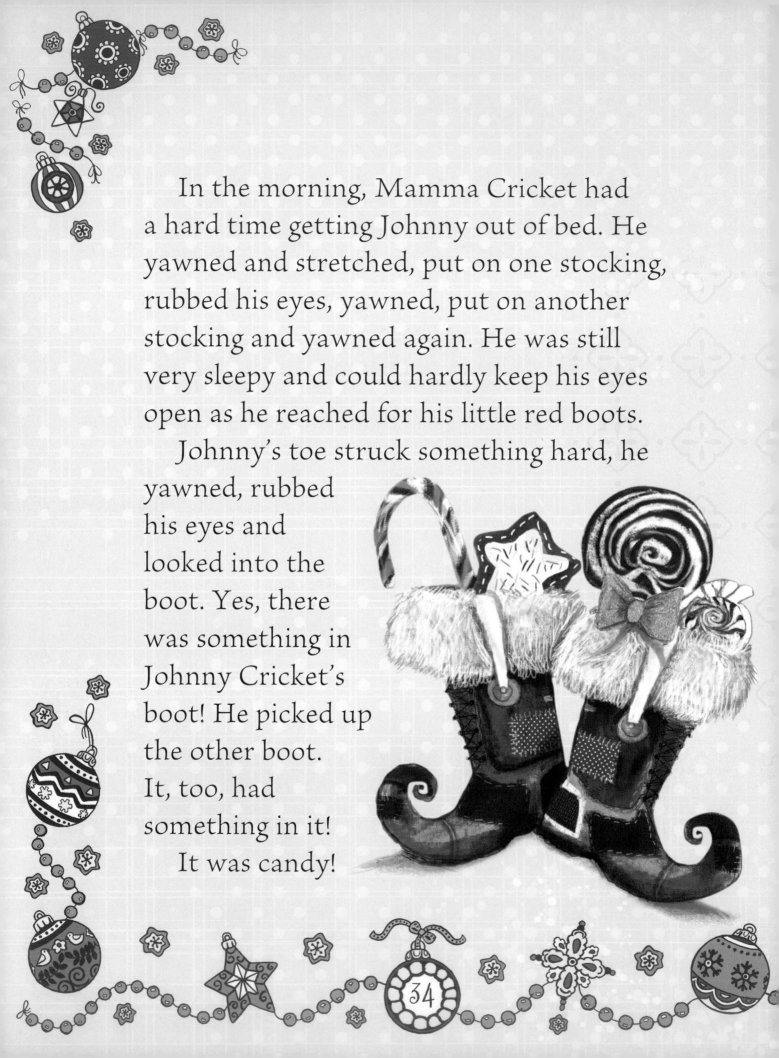

How Johnny Cricket Saw Santa Claus

With a loud cry for such a little cricket, Johnny rushed to the kitchen and showed Mamma Cricket.

And then Johnny Cricket told Mamma Cricket all about his exciting adventure the night before.

Mamma Cricket called Papa Cricket and they both had a laugh when Johnny told how startled he had been at the old man with the white whiskers who filled the stockings in front of the fireplace.

"Why, Johnny!" said Mamma and Papa Cricket. "Don't you know? That was Santa Claus. We have watched him every Christmas for the last four years fill the stockings. Santa Claus saw your little red boots and filled them with candy, too. If you crawl through the crack into the fireplace you will see the children of the

people who own this big house playing with all the presents that Santa Claus left them." And, sure enough, it was so.

A Visit from St Nicholas

By Clement Clarke Moore

’Twas the night before Christmas, when all through the house
Not a creature was stirring, not even a mouse;
The stockings were hung by the chimney with care,
In hopes that St Nicholas soon would be there.

The children were nestled all snug in their beds,
While visions of sugar-plums danced in their heads.
And mamma in her ’kerchief, and I in my cap,
Had just settled our brains for a long winter’s nap.

When out on the lawn there arose such a clatter,

I sprang from the bed to see what was the matter.

Away to the window I flew like a flash,

Tore open the shutters and threw up the sash.

The moon on the breast of the new-fallen snow

Gave the lustre of midday to objects below.

When, what to my wondering eyes should appear,

But a miniature sleigh, and eight tiny reindeer.

With a little old driver, so lively and quick,

I knew in a moment it must be St Nick.

More rapid than eagles his coursers they came,

And he whistled, and shouted, and called them by name!

"Now, Dasher! Now, Dancer! Now, Prancer and Vixen!

On, Comet! On, Cupid! On, on Donner and Blitzen!

To the top of the porch! To the top of the wall!

Now dash away! Dash away! Dash away all!"

A Visit from St Nicholas

As dry leaves that before the wild hurricane fly,
When they meet with an obstacle, mount to the sky.
So up to the house-top the coursers they flew,
With the sleigh full of toys, and St Nicholas too.

And then, in a twinkling, I heard on the roof
The prancing and pawing of each little hoof.
As I drew in my head, and was turning around,
Down the chimney St Nicholas came with a bound.

He was dressed all in fur, from his head to his foot,
And his clothes were all tarnished with ashes and soot.
A bundle of toys he had flung on his back,
And he looked like a peddler, just opening his pack.

His eyes – how they twinkled! His dimples how merry!
His cheeks were like roses, his nose like a cherry!
His droll little mouth was drawn up like a bow,
And the beard of his chin was as white as the snow.

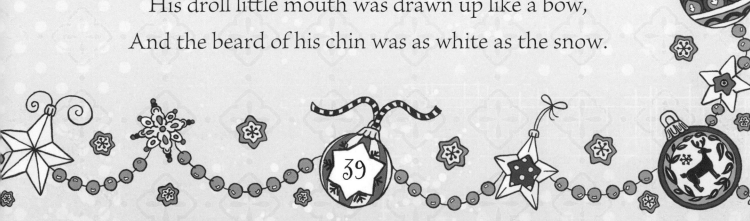

The stump of a pipe he held tight in his teeth,

And the smoke it encircled his head like a wreath.

He had a broad face and a little round belly,

That shook when he laughed, like a bowlful of jelly!

He was chubby and plump, a right jolly old elf,

And I laughed when I saw him, in spite of myself!

A wink of his eye and a twist of his head,

Soon gave me to know I had nothing to dread.

He spoke not a word, but went straight to his work,

And filled all the stockings, then turned with a jerk.

And laying his finger aside of his nose,

And giving a nod, up the chimney he rose!

He sprang to his sleigh, to his team gave a whistle,

And away they all flew like the down of a thistle.

But I heard him exclaim, 'ere he drove out of sight,

"Happy Christmas to all, and to all a good night!"